Zoey AND SASSAFRAS

CATERFLIES AND ICE

THE
INNOVATION
PRESS

READ THE REST OF THE SERIES

for activities and more visit

ZOEYANDSASSAFRAS.COM

TABLE OF CONTENTS

FOR SYLVIE AND GRAHAM — ML
FOR GOOSE AND BUBS — AC

Audience: Grades K-5.
LCCN 2017906949
ISBN 9781943147342; ISBN 9781943147359; ISBN 9781943147366

Published by The Innovation Press
1001 4th Avenue, Suite 3200 Seattle, WA 98154
www.theinnovationpress.com

Printed and bound by Worzalla
Production Date: September 2017 | Plant Location: Stevens Point, Wisconsin

Cover design by Nicole LaRue | Book layout by Kerry Ellis

PROLOGUE

These days my cat Sassafras and I are always desperately hoping we'll hear our barn doorbell.

I know most people are excited to hear their doorbell ring. It might mean a present or package delivery, or a friend showing up to play. But our doorbell is even more exciting than that. Because it's a *magic* doorbell. When it rings, it means there's a magical animal waiting outside our barn. A magical animal who needs our help.

My mom's been helping them basically her whole life. And now *I* get to help too ...

SPRING SNOW

CHAPTER 1

A shower of powdery crystals glittered in the air and fell on my face.

Brrrr. I grinned.

Snow. Is. Awesome. And this snow was especially awesome because it was a surprise spring snow. I thought it would be almost a year before I saw snow again.

As I bent down to grab another armful of the powdery white fluff blanketing the lawn, I heard a *thump* behind me.

I turned to see a little orange face smooshed against the window.

Mrrrfff.

Poor Sassafras. He hates water. And because snow melts into water when his warm kitty paw touches it? Yeah. He pretty much hates snow as much as I love it.

Mrrrfff. *Thump.*

I trudged over and put my hand against the windowpane. Inside, Sassafras raised his paw to the same spot. Hmmmm...

"Wait a minute, Sassafras. Let me find my Thinking Goggles. There's gotta be a way for you to play outside and not get wet!"

I ran off to our barn and peeked inside. There they were—next to some of my mom's old science journals.

I grabbed my Thinking Goggles, pausing for a moment to run my hand over a photo in one of the journals. My mom's notes said the creature in the photo was a fweep (which is very fun to say), and I could feel its soft-as-silk fur through the photo. I smiled. The photos of magical animals always amazed me. Mom gave me my own camera, and I'm allowed to take one photo of each magical creature I help. I like to add them to my science journal with my notes. Because every photo saves a bit of magic with it, it's a great way to remember the sweet magical friends I've made.

I popped the Thinking Goggles on my head, made sure they were close to my brain (to give me awesome ideas quickly), and ran back to my poor sad cat in the window.

SNOWSHOES
CHAPTER 2

Sassafras saw the Thinking Goggles on my head and perked up.

Now I just needed to think. Hmmm. Maybe making a snow angel would help! The cold snow tickled the back of my head as I swooshed my arms and legs back and forth. The first idea that popped into my head cracked me up. I could put Sassafras inside a giant plastic ball. As he walked, the ball would roll and his little paws would never get wet! OK, maybe he wouldn't go for that. But it did sound pretty fun. "Good one, Thinking Goggles." I giggled as I finished making a snow angel.

I stood up and brushed myself off, and a tiny bit of snow dust sneaked its way into my boot. I shivered. A second solution popped into my head. "Oooh! I like it!" I exclaimed and then ran for the kitchen door.

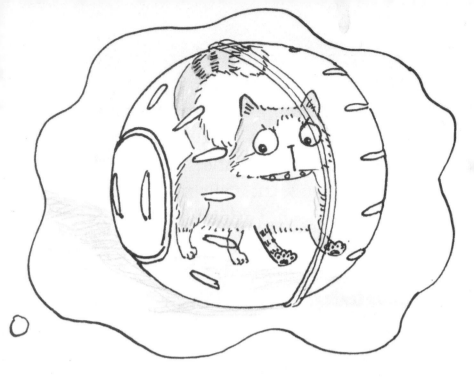

I left my boots by the door and ran to scoop up my cat. "Sassafras, I have a plan!" I told him. He purred and bumped his head against mine. "We just need to ask Mom for some help and I think we'll be all set!"

"Ask me what?" my mom said as she entered the room, leafing through the mail.

"I have a great idea. You know how

Sassafras hates the snow?"

"Mmm-hmm."

"I'll make him little tiny snowshoes! That way he can play in the snow, but his paws will stay dry. I put my Thinking Goggles on, and after the first idea, I remembered that Xander's dog wears little Velcro snowshoes when his

family hikes in the snow."

"Hmmm." Mom wrinkled her nose a little. "Do you think he'd wear them?"

I looked deep into Sassafras' eyes. "Sassafras. If I make you snowshoes so your paws won't get wet, will you wear them?"

Sassafras looked deep into my eyes. Then he licked my nose.

Mom and I both laughed.

"Can we try making them, Mom? Pleeease?"

"OK, let's give it a try. But don't be upset if he won't wear them."

"I promise! Do you have any waterproof fabric? And can you help me with the sewing machine, pleeeease?" I smiled sweetly at my mom.

She grinned back and waved for me to follow her. "Let's see what I've got in the hall closet. Thankfully, we won't need much material—Sassafras has such little paws!"

I set Sassafras down and we both followed Mom.

"Huh," Mom said as she rummaged through the fabric scraps. "I'm not seeing any waterproof fabric in here. And I only have a little bit of Velcro left." She held up a tiny square.

"Oooh, Velcro would be perfect, but that's only enough for one shoe. I don't think he'd enjoy having to balance on one foot!"

"I have to go to the grocery store anyway. Why don't we make a list of supplies you need, and I'll make a quick stop at the fabric store while I'm out?"

"Thanks, Mom!" I gave her a big hug.

We made the list, and Mom left. Sassafras curled up in my lap and I sketched a few different cat snowshoe designs while we waited for her to get back. Then we heard it.

The magic doorbell!

HELP!

CHAPTER 3

Sassafras and I looked at each other, and then we launched off the couch and ran for the kitchen door. I tossed on my boots and hollered, "I'll be right back, Dad! Just going out to the barn to play!"

My dad called back an OK as I opened the door and plunged into the sparkling snow.

Right on my heels, Sassafras took two big steps into the snow. Then he froze. And hissed. And then bolted back into the house, wiggling and bouncing and shaking each paw in disgust.

"Oh, Sassafras!" I sighed. "Why don't you sit this one out? I'll be right back."

I gave him a quick hug and dashed to the barn. I was buzzing with excitement. What kind of magical animal would be here this time? Maybe a fweep? Or another baby dragon? I ran through the barn and quickly opened the back door.

Nothing. Could it have been a false alarm? Sometimes magical animals are really small. Maybe I could see it if I got closer?

I bent down, but all I saw was white snow. Except that some of the snow had *something* on it. What were those pink dots?

I reached out and poked them with my finger.

"Whoa!" I yelped as I jumped backward. Umm, did that pile of snow just *hiss* at me?

The little hill of snow bloomed right before my eyes. At the center were two tiny, fuzzy green bodies with white wings—and their little faces were looking up at me.

I rubbed my eyes. Whoooooaa. They looked like miniature six-legged green cats, with big butterfly wings as white as snow . . . and with tiny pink dots!

"Are you . . . butterflies?" I whispered.

The two winged creatures looked at

each other and then up at me. "No. Do we look like butterflies?" one asked, and then uncurled a long tongue and cleaned one of its furry paws.

"We are caterflies, obviously," added the second creature as it shook its furry body, "and we are very wet and very c-c-c-cold! Do you have someplace warm and dry for us?"

I nodded and carefully moved the tiny, furry caterflies to a desk in the barn. I brought back a little space heater and

turned it on. The caterflies closed their eyes and looked as if they were smiling. They even started . . . purring? Then one caterfly popped up and bopped the other caterfly on the head with its paw.

"Heyyyy!" growled the bopped caterfly.

The first caterfly put four of its six paws on its hips. "We can't forget why we are here!"

At this, both caterflies stood and faced me. "This is the barn where we come for help, yes? And you are the human that

helps us?" one of them asked.

I nodded. I thought they'd just needed my help getting warm. But apparently they had a bigger problem! "My name is Zoey, and I'm happy to help you. Why don't you start by telling me what's wrong?"

"It's this awful cold." The first caterfly paced back and forth on the desk. "We laid our eggs on our host plants like we do every spring. We busied ourselves tending to the plants and getting ready for our eggs to hatch. And then instead of getting warmer like it always does, it got colder!

And this horrid snow started falling!"

The second caterfly jumped in. "Our eggs aren't supposed to be in snow. We panicked. Our host plants grow by the entrance to a small cave not far from here. We decided to move the eggs into the cave to keep them warm."

A small cave not far from here? Ohhhh. I was pretty sure I knew what cave they were talking about. I looked more closely at the colors of their bodies and the patterns on their wings and realized something.

"Is your host plant catnip?" I asked.

"But of course," replied the second caterfly.

The caterflies looked like the catnip plants and flowers so they could easily hide from predators! What great camouflage. They really did look like the catnip that grew by that cave. Every time we walked past there, Sassafras became a purring, drooling mess from all the wild catnip. We hadn't been since summer because it can get a bit muddy, and mud is slippery! I'd often wished the cave was big enough for me to go inside, but it was small . . . about the size of Sassafras. I worried that if I poked my arm inside, I'd scare something that might bite me!

The first caterfly cleared its throat to get my attention. "After we moved the eggs into the cave, I pointed out that predators might look for caves to keep warm. And they'd eat our eggs if they found them!"

"And then I had the idea to hide the eggs behind a little waterfall," the second caterfly whispered as it hung its head sadly.

The first caterfly lovingly bumped its head against the second, who clearly felt bad about whatever had happened with the waterfall. "It wasn't your fault," it said to its friend.

Here I interrupted both of them. "Wait—there's a waterfall inside the cave?

And what happened?"

Looking back at me, the first caterfly continued, "At the back of the cave, a small waterfall runs out to the plants. It's probably why our host plants grow so well there. We found a little nook in the rocks behind the falling water and hid the eggs there. We figured no predator would look

behind the waterfall. But we didn't realize it would get colder. We didn't realize the water would freeze!"

I put a hand to my mouth. "Oh no! Are your eggs trapped behind the frozen waterfall?"

The caterflies nodded sadly.

The first caterfly said, "We are so worried about our eggs. They might get too cold."

This was a real emergency! We couldn't let those eggs freeze. I needed an idea. And fast. I needed my Thinking Goggles!

I turned to look for them and then realized they were still on my head from earlier. Hah!

"Don't worry, caterflies. We'll figure out a way to save your babies! Let me think for a minute. We need to melt the ice. Ice, ice, ice . . ." I muttered as I tapped my Thinking Goggles.

Hot water would work, but how could I take enough hot water through the forest to the cave? I could bring a thermos, I guess, but I didn't know how much ice there was. There must be another way to melt ice. Come on, Thinking Goggles!

I started to feel warm. Almost like summer warm. Huh? Ohhhh! I get it! One of my favorite summer activities is an ice excavation. My mom takes a bunch of little trinkets and toys and adds them to a container. Then she fills the entire container with water and freezes it. The next day she pops out the chunk of ice and all the toys are frozen inside. I get the treasures out one by one using a paintbrush, pipette, water, and–

SALT. Of course! And even better, salt would be super easy to take to the forest.

"Yes!" I exclaimed out loud. The caterflies jumped. "Oh, I didn't mean to scare you! I have a plan. But first I need to grab some supplies and ask my dad if I can go."

The caterflies started to come with me.

"Ummm, he can't see you guys. It'll freak him out if I'm talking to invisible things. So maybe I'll just leave you here by the heater for a minute. Is that OK?"

The caterflies looked at each other and nodded. "We love the heater." They both purred loudly.

I giggled and then dashed back home. Hopefully Dad would let me go to the forest–I had some caterfly eggs to rescue!

PLEASE?
CHAPTER 4

The door banged as I came back in the house.

"Back already, Zoey? Did you get too cold?" Dad called out.

I tossed my boots by the kitchen door. "No, not too cold. Ummm, can I go out into the forest?"

Dad looked out the window and frowned. "I don't know . . . it's pretty cold out. And it's getting late in the afternoon. Maybe in a few days? I think it's supposed to warm up later in the week."

Oh no. The eggs weren't supposed to be cold, and they were already behind ice. I didn't know how many more hours they could stand the cold. There was no way they could make it a few *days*.

"Pleeeease? I don't think it's supposed to snow anymore today, right? I'll bundle

up. I'll even wear gloves! I just need to check on something in the forest. It's not that far. I could be super quick?" I gave him my sweetest and most desperate smile.

Dad looked out the window again and checked his watch and sighed.

"OK. But I want you back in twenty minutes."

I nodded.

"Twenty minutes and no more," he repeated, raising an eyebrow at me.

"I promise! I just need to grab a few things. I'll be super-duper fast. Thank you, Dad!" I said as I hugged him.

I went straight to the kitchen and dug through our cabinet until I found our only thermos. I filled it with hot water and grabbed the salt from the pantry. I got my backpack from the living room, dumped my school stuff on the floor, and packed the thermos and salt into the bag. I just needed one more thing . . .

I knelt down to Sassafras. "Hey buddy, I have a job for you! There are some really sweet and really cold little caterflies in the barn that need our help. Can you be their heater for our trip into the forest? I can carry you in the backpack so you don't get wet." I scratched under his chin to sweeten the deal.

Sassafras looked from the door to the backpack and back again. Then he walked over to the backpack and let out a big sigh.

Backpack ride it is! I shoved one of my sweaters into the backpack to make a cushion for Sassafras and then squeezed him in. I left the top part unzipped so he could see and then slowly put on my backpack full of cat, salt, and water. Oof. That was heavy. Good thing I was strong.

"Now all we need are the caterflies!" I whispered over my shoulder and tromped through the snow to the barn.

MEET THE CATERFLIES
CHAPTER 5

I opened the barn door and smiled at the loud rumbles of happy caterflies purring.

When I got to the desk, Sassafras hopped out of my backpack. The loud *thump* he made as he landed startled the caterflies.

Their eyes got huge and they fluttered over with their six furry legs stretched out to hug Sassafras.

"Ohhhhhhhh, what is this?!" both

caterflies asked as they hovered around him.

"This is my cat, Sassafras," I replied proudly.

Sassafras looked from me to the caterflies and back again and took a small step backward.

I ruffled Sassafras' fur. "It's OK. These are the caterflies I was telling you about. They won't hurt you."

One of the caterflies landed by
Sassafras' front paw and leaned its little
cheek against his fur and sighed. "You
have brought us a cat!"

The second caterfly lovingly bopped
its head against Sassafras' other front paw.
"He is so warm. Oh, thank you!"

Sassafras' ears went sideways, and he
looked up at me questioningly.

"Pleeeeease, Sass? We've got to hurry!"

He let out another big sigh and bent down. The caterflies hopped on and nestled into his fur. They immediately started purring.

I clapped my hands in victory. This was so cute! It would make a great photo, but we were in too big of a hurry. I'd have to wait until later.

Gently, I placed the fluffy heap of cat plus two caterflies into my backpack.

How much time did I have left? I glanced at my watch. Only fifteen minutes before Sassafras and I needed to be back home. I walked as fast as I could straight toward the caterflies' cave.

ICE!
CHAPTER 6

I knew I'd found the right cave as soon as we got there. Just inside the entrance I could see a pile of caterflies huddled together like a tiny mountain of white snow with little pink dots. I set my backpack on a nearby rock, and the caterflies flew from Sassafras' fur into the cave.

Sassafras looked around at the snow and decided to stay in the backpack.

I didn't have much time, so I dug

around in the backpack for the thermos while Sassafras grumbled. I took it to the mouth of the tiny cave and peeked in. It was a little hard to see, but I could make out a shiny layer of ice where the waterfall had frozen.

The two caterflies woke up the rest of the caterflies in the cave and told them about their adventure to and from the barn that morning. It ended with them pointing to me, saying, "That's Zoey. She's going to rescue our eggs!"

The cave of caterflies cheered.

Then the two caterflies continued, "Zoey has a cat. A real live cat. He's ever so warm. Come see!"

All the caterflies rushed to the front of the cave and peered out.

"Ooooooooh!" they said at once. And then one, and another, and then all the caterflies launched into the air and landed on my cat. They snuggled down into his fur and began to purr.

I wished I had my camera because all I could see was Sassafras' face peeking out from a mound of white wings. I thought he would be nervous, but he looked like he was smiling. Maybe dozens of tiny purring cats snuggling happily against you is a good recipe for happiness.

I glanced at my watch. Oh no! I only had a few minutes left.

After unscrewing the lid of the thermos, I was relieved to see steam coming from the water inside. Still hot. Phew.

I reached into the cave and splashed the water on the wall of ice that trapped the caterfly eggs. The ice made crackling noises, and I could see some lines forming, but it wasn't enough.

Good thing I'd also brought the salt. I wouldn't be able to come back until tomorrow, so I figured it was best to just use all of it now. It should definitely be enough to melt that ice!

I pulled my glove off with my teeth and poured a ton of salt into my open hand. Then I rubbed the salt as best I could all over the ice. When I was done, the ice had a nice layer of salt on it. With my ear to the cave, I could hear more ice crackling (though it was a little hard to hear over all the purring going on behind me).

I looked at my watch again and my heart jumped into my throat. We had to leave for home right now!

"Caterflies! I'm sorry, but we've really got to go. My dad will be worried if I'm home late. I think the ice should melt now with the salt on it. I'll be back

tomorrow morning to check on you, and I'll bring my mom in case the ice doesn't melt."

The caterflies flew up and circled around my head, thanking me. I giggled.

They sure were cute little creatures. "See you tomorrow, Zoey!" they cheered as they flew into their cave for the night.

I snapped up Sassafras in the backpack. "Hold on tight, Sass!"

Sassafras hunkered down, and I ran for home.

JUST IN TIME

CHAPTER 7

I burst through the door, set my Sassafras backpack down gently, and put my hands on my knees, panting. My dad rounded the corner three seconds later.

"Ah, good! You're home. Thank you for being responsible. I was starting to worry I shouldn't have sent you out so late in the afternoon."

"Thanks . . . Dad . . ." I huffed out. "I'm . . . glad . . . I . . . got to go."

Sassafras' ears perked up, and his head

spun toward the front door a moment before I heard it open. Mom!

"Brrrr, it's getting cold out there," Mom said as she carried two grocery bags and a small plastic bag into the kitchen. She paused when she saw me. "What have you been up to?"

"Uhhhh, I needed to do something," I winked a few times for good measure, "out in the forest."

"Something in the forest? OHH!" my

mom said as she finally realized what I was hinting at.

"I can help Mom put these away, Dad," I chirped.

"OK, I'll leave you to it then," Dad said as he left the kitchen.

"Oh, Mom!" I whispered. "Have you ever seen caterflies? They are SO cute! Their eggs were trapped behind ice but I rescued them . . . at least, I'm pretty sure I did. I had to rush home. But can

we go check and make sure they're OK tomorrow? First thing? Right after I wake up?"

Mom laughed. "They sound adorable. I can't wait to meet them! Great work helping them and yes, let's go first thing in the morning. I also got you this," and she slid a bag over to me.

I opened it and squealed. "Fabric for Sassafras' snowshoes! Yessss! Thank you!"

"Go grab your sketches, and we can get these ready for Sassafras before tomorrow morning's adventure," Mom said as she put away the last of the groceries. I hurried off to grab my plans for the coolest cat shoes ever. If we worked quickly, Sassafras could wear them to visit the caterflies tomorrow!

NOT MORE!
CHAPTER 8

I woke up early and shivered. I pulled a warm Sassafras onto my chest and he purred. Then I remembered the caterflies and leaped out of bed. Sassafras jumped sideways and landed with his tail poofed up.

"Sorry, Sass!" I ruffled his fur. "The caterflies! We need to check on them!"

"Meow!" exclaimed Sassafras, and he ran for the kitchen.

Mom was sitting at the table with a sad

look on her face. She shook her head.

I gulped. "What's wrong, Mom?"

Mom slowly turned to the window. Wild gusts of wind were flinging giant flakes of snow this way and that. I could barely make out the forest through the blinding whiteness of the falling snow. My heart sank. We couldn't go out in the woods in this weather. It would be too dangerous because snow and wind can work together to make tree branches snap.

"I'm sure they'll be fine, Zoey," Mom said. "There's just a bit more of this spring snowstorm that needs to work its way through. The forecast says it should be over by tomorrow. But today we need to sit tight and wait it out."

I walked to the kitchen counter and peered out the window. The snow was really coming down. I could barely see the forest through all the snowflakes.

"I know what will cheer you up!" Mom plopped four little shoes onto the counter in front of me. "I put the finishing touches on these after you fell asleep. Are you ready to test them out on our brave kitty?"

I still felt sad about the caterflies, but I couldn't help smiling at the tiny Sassafras snowshoes! I sat down on the ground and Sassafras came over and sniffed at them suspiciously.

"These will be great, Sass. Just you wait and see." I plunked him in my lap, slipped a shoe on each paw, and attached each one with Velcro so they wouldn't fall off. Time to see if they worked!

Sassafras took a step and stopped. He wrinkled his nose. Then he took another step. He lifted a paw and sniffed at the shoe. Then he started prancing. He held his head high and fluffed up his tail and took fancy steps around the kitchen. Mom and I bent over laughing.

Dad peeked his head in and took one look at Sassafras and laughed so hard, a

tear rolled down his cheek!

After our laughter died down, Dad looked out the window and let out a big breath.

His shoulders slumped. "I guess it's time to start shoveling the walkway and driveway."

A huge grin spread across my face. I knew how to make this easier for my dad! "But Dad, just use some salt! Salt will melt the snow and ice. Then you don't have to

work so hard shoveling!"

Mom patted my head. "That's a great idea, Zoey, and while salt would change the freezing point of the water and melt the ice, it's best if Dad does it the good old-fashioned way. Salt can damage plants, and it's not great for the environment. Maybe we can make some hot cocoa for him once he's done." Then she looked at my face. "Oh, honey, what's wrong?"

I cleared my throat. I didn't want to ask, but I needed to know. "The salt. You said it can damage plants?"

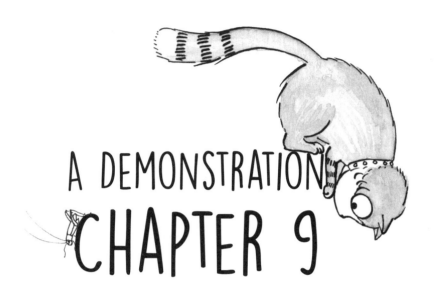

A DEMONSTRATION
CHAPTER 9

Mom cleared off the kitchen counter. "Can you grab two bowls that are the same size and a measuring cup, Zoey?"

Mom said the best way to explain what salt does to plants was to do a science *demo* (that's short for demonstration). I set the bowls and measuring cup next to our saltshaker, and Mom brought several thin circles she'd sliced from a potato. They looked like weirdly flat and juicy potato chips.

Mom cleared her throat. "OK, so let's see what happens when we add salt to one potato slice and not another. Remember, when we do an experiment, we always—"

"Change one thing! And keep everything else the same!" I interrupted, and Mom laughed.

"Exactly, so we're changing . . ."

"Salt! So we should do the same-sized potato slices in each bowl, and add the same amount of water to both."

"Excellent!" My mom smiled and

handed me the measuring cup. The bowls were pretty big, so I decided to add two cups of water to each. Then I chose two thin potato slices that looked identical and put one in each bowl.

Mom unscrewed the lid to the saltshaker and handed it to me.

"All of it?" I asked.

She nodded. I poured all of the salt into just one of the bowls and stirred the water, salt, and potato slice together.

"Are you sure about this?" I asked, looking into the bowl. "It's just a slice of potato, not a plant." A catnip plant and a potato slice seemed pretty different to me. So maybe the catnip plants would be just fine.

"In this demo, the slice represents the whole plant. So even though the potato slice is just a part of a potato plant, it'll show you what all the parts of any plant would do in this much salty water."

Oh. Well . . . maybe the potato slice wouldn't change much? I hoped. I really wanted the catnip plants to be fine. Once the caterfly eggs hatched, they'd be hungry for those leaves!

Mom set a timer for thirty minutes. "Now we wait."

RUBBERY POTATOES
CHAPTER 10

Sassafras and I smooshed our noses against the window, staring at the never-ending snowstorm, when the kitchen timer went off. We dashed into the kitchen, eager to see what had happened to our potato slices. Sassafras was so curious, he even jumped on the counter to see.

"Sassafras!" my mom scolded as she joined us.

Sassafras lowered his head and jumped back down.

I picked up the potato slice that was in plain water first and bent down to show him. He took a sniff but leaped backward as a water drop fell from the potato.

"It feels the same, I think," I gave it a poke. "Maybe a little stronger? It seems harder to bend now."

Mom nodded.

Next I plunged my hand into the salty water. My fingers touched the potato slice, and I made a face. I pulled it out and knelt down. "This one is gross, Sassafras." I wiggled it between my hands to show him. "It feels rubbery." I looked up at Mom. "What does that mean?"

"Things like to be equal when they can," she said as she sat down at our kitchen table. She picked up the saltwater potato slice. "More salt was outside the potato than inside the potato itself. To even out the saltiness, water moved out of the potato. But only a little water has moved out so far. We'll leave it overnight, and you'll see a big difference tomorrow morning. Water will keep moving out

of the potato to make the saltiness more equal."

I picked up the plain water potato slice. "So this one was pretty even already? That's why the water didn't have to move a bunch here?"

Mom nodded. "So, can you figure out what saltwater might do to a whole plant?"

I poked the rubbery potato slice as I thought out loud.

"If there's salt around a plant, and plants try to make things even by moving water . . . that means . . ." I gasped. Oh no.

"What's wrong, honey?"

I looked down at my feet. "I, um, made a mistake, Mom. With the caterflies. I dumped a ton of salt on the ice to make it melt faster. I was worried about the eggs freezing!" I slowly picked up the rubbery potato slice. "Will the catnip host plants look like this tomorrow? Because if they do . . . what are the baby caterflies going to eat once they hatch?"

Mom rubbed my back. "Oh, honey. We all make mistakes. You never know, the salt might not have made it very far. We'll have to wait and see. Try to take your mind off it. Whatever's happened, we'll figure it out tomorrow."

I felt like tomorrow would take forever to get here! Maybe Mom was right and I should keep myself busy so I wouldn't worry as much. While Mom made hot cocoa, I grabbed my science journal and decided I'd write down everything I'd learned about the caterflies so far:

CATERFLIES

What I know:

- they lay eggs
- eggs can't get too cold
- eggs hatch into caterpillars
- caterpillars eat catnip (host plant).

Then I added all the caterfly things I still wondered about:

CATERFLIES

What I wonder.
- do they make a chrysalis?

- what do the adult caterflies eat?
- can the caterpillars talk?
- can Sassafras understand them?

As I wrote and sipped hot cocoa with Sassafras purring in my lap, I felt a little better. Maybe the plants wouldn't be as bad as the potato after all.

FINALLY!
CHAPTER 11

"Psssssst!"

My eyes sprang open. What was that weird noise? I turned my head and almost crashed into my mom's face. I jumped.

My mom laughed. "Sorry to startle you, sweetie!" She lifted a hand to show me a fully packed backpack. "I told your dad we had cabin fever and needed to go for an early morning hike."

I had to squint because it was so bright in my room. Wait a second! Bright! Sun!

"It's sunny!" I exclaimed.

"Yep." Mom nodded. "The news said that all the snow should melt this afternoon. That wild storm has finally passed, and it's going to warm up today."

I listened as I shoved on my snow gear.

"But this morning it's 31 degrees out," Mom continued. "Do you remember what that means?"

I nodded. "Water has a freezing point of 32 degrees. Since 31 degrees is below that, everything will be frozen. But once it's above 32 degrees, the water won't stay frozen ... so the ice and snow will melt?"

Mom smiled. "You got it! It's supposed to be 55 by this afternoon, so it will seem downright hot!"

We paused briefly in the kitchen where I grabbed a piece of buttered toast my mom had made for breakfast on the go. Sassafras filled his cheeks

with cat food and then waited patiently to be outfitted with his cat snowshoes.

This time a prancing Sassafras led the way. I tried to calm my hammering heart. I really hoped the plants would be OK. And the caterflies and their eggs were safe!

I slowed down as the catnip plants came into view. Oh no. All the catnip plants around the cave entrance had wilted. Several of the leaves were brown. What had I done?

A tear rolled down my cheek. What would the caterflies do? Their babies needed to eat the host plant—and lots of it— as soon as they hatched. Only a few plants were left. Would their baby caterpillars starve because of my mistake?

Mom came over and put a hand under my chin. She tilted my face up to hers. "Don't worry, sweetheart. I have a few tricks up my sleeve. But first, let's find the caterflies!"

I wiped the snow off a nearby rock
with my glove, and Sassafras sat down and
waited. He kept glancing at the catnip,
but he knew we needed to save it for the
caterflies. I was proud of him—it must have
been like sitting in a candy shop and not
eating any of the candy!

The three of us looked around, but
there was no sign of the caterflies. I was
terrified to walk closer to the cave—what if
I accidentally stepped on one?

Sassafras sniffed the air and let out a loud "Meeeeooooowwwww."

I spotted some movement near the cave entrance. I tapped Mom's shoulder and pointed. What looked like a small mound of snow began to quake . . . and shake . . . and then it exploded into a dozen caterflies. A small flock flew straight toward Sassafras.

He looked at me with big eyes. Floomp! Ten caterflies instantly coated him. His whole body seemed to vibrate with caterfly purrs.

Over the loud rumbling purrs, I managed to hear them say, "You brought us a Sassafras! It is so warm! Thank you!"

I knelt down. "I was so worried about you. There was too much wind and snow to come yesterday. Is everyone OK?"

One of the caterflies that came to our barn left Sassafras and landed on my wrist. "Your tricks worked, and the ice cracked.

We rescued our eggs! But then the snow and wind started again. We didn't want them to get trapped a second time, so we set them on a rock by the front of the cave and all piled on to protect them. We were so happy to see the sun this morning! But what is wrong with our plants?"

I sighed. "I made a mistake using the salt. It melted the ice, but it hurt your

plants. Salt makes water leave the plants, which is why they wilted and turned brown. I am so sorry. I didn't know it would do that!" Another tear slid down my cheek.

The caterfly rubbed its face against my wrist and purred lightly. "It's OK, Zoey. You rescued our eggs. Besides, a few plants still look healthy. That might be enough for our caterpillars once they hatch."

I looked over the field of catnip plants. About half of them were damaged. I shook

my head. It didn't look like enough.

Mom put her arm around my shoulder.

"We need more catnip plants," I said. "I don't think what's left will be enough to feed the baby caterpillars."

Mom nodded. "What do you think we should do?"

I reached into my backpack and popped on my Thinking Goggles. We needed more plants . . . more plants . . .

hmmmm. The first word that popped into my head was seeds. But there weren't any flowers yet and seeds take an awfully long time to grow. The next word was my friend Sophie. Sophie? Really, Thinking Goggles? I mean, it would be fun to play with her later, but . . . OH!

"The African violets!" I practically shouted.

Mom smiled.

Before I got distracted by the snow, I'd been working on a surprise for my friends in our greenhouse. My mom showed me a trick where I could clip leaves from our African violet plant and plant the stems in the soil. The stems of that plant can grow roots, which is super weird. And amazing. After the leaves grow into plants, I can give them to my friends at the end of the year. "Can catnip stems grow roots, too? Could we clip off leaves from the catnip and plant them in soil to make new plants in our greenhouse?"

"That sounds like an excellent plan! And you're right. Herbs like catnip can do exactly what the African violets do—grow new plants from part of the original plant."

I raised the caterfly on my wrist up to my face. "How would you feel about moving to our greenhouse for a few weeks?"

"A greenhouse? Does it have a Sassafras?" the caterfly asked.

"It does have a Sassafras. And it's nice and warm." With one finger, I gently petted the head of the caterfly.

"Warm! And a Sassafras! Yes!" exclaimed the caterfly.

"Then let's get to work," Mom said. She walked to a healthy catnip plant and waved me over. "Zoey, you'll need to clip off the ends of the plants here," she said, pointing to the tip of a stem with about five new leaves unfurling, "and put them in this bag."

Once I'd collected the clippings, we headed back to the greenhouse, caterflies and all.

MAGIC?

CHAPTER 12

Mom set out several pots, a bag of potting soil, a watering can, and the bag full of my catnip clippings. I planted the stems just like I'd done with the African violet leaves for my friends. As we worked, Mom explained that not all plants grow well from pieces—only certain kinds, like aloe or herbs. I felt pretty lucky that catnip was one of those plants!

When I was done, I stood back to admire my work. "Will this be enough,

Mom? Won't the caterflies need to eat
these?"

A caterfly landed on my wrist. "Silly
Zoey. We don't eat plants. Blech! Only
caterpillars like the taste of them. We
drink delicious nectar from flowers. Like
butterflies!"

"Ooooooh, nectar!" several caterflies
purred.

I looked around the greenhouse. "But

we don't have any flowering plants. How will you eat?"

"Well, we usually drink nectar from the forest flowers, but we know a trick." The caterflies giggled. "If we want to try different nectar, we sneak into garden stores. It doesn't hurt the flowers. There's plenty of food there. And it's warm inside!" purred the caterfly on my wrist. Then it popped into the air and flew to the greenhouse roof. "We can come and

go through here. It's useful to be small
sometimes!"

The caterfly fluttered back to Sassafras,
who was thrilled at the attention from the
tiny creatures. Mom and I worked together
to add the catnip stems to the different
pots. When we finished, we stepped back
and grinned. Sassafras had curled up on
the workbench and was snoring lightly.
And so were the dozen caterflies on his
back. Mom tenderly placed the eggs at
the bottom of a new catnip plant, and we
tiptoed out of the greenhouse.

IT'S TIME

CHAPTER 13

Sassafras and I laughed as we ran through the green grass in our yard. The sun shone down on our faces, and the caterflies flitted happily through the warm spring air while we played another game of tag. The caterflies were really fast so it wasn't a fair game (they always won), but we enjoyed it anyway.

I flopped on the ground to catch my breath, and Sassafras jumped on my stomach. A pile of giggling caterflies soon joined him. I closed my eyes and smiled as the sun warmed my face, when Sassafras let out a meow.

"What is it, buddy?" I asked, ruffling his fur. I peeked with one eye and saw my mom coming over. She had a bucket and her gardening clothes on.

I propped myself up on my elbows.

"It's time," she said.

I knew this was coming. "Are you sure they can't stay a little bit longer?" I whined.

"We need to replant the catnip plants. They're getting too big for their pots. Plus, the caterfly eggs are due to hatch any day now. You don't want the caterpillars growing up inside a greenhouse, do you? Not when they could grow up seeing this beautiful sky every day?" Mom lifted her arms out, tilted her head back, and smiled with eyes closed toward the sun.

She had a point. It was beautiful out here.

"You can still visit them, you know," she added.

I sighed and hauled myself up. The caterflies fluttered around my head. "It's time! It's time!" they chirped. They were so excited. I tried my best to be happy for them as I followed my mom back to the greenhouse.

After we filled the wagon with supplies, I ran into the house and grabbed my backpack with my camera and science journal. I couldn't keep the caterflies, but I could at least take a photo of them.

I led the way to the catnip field, and Sassafras trotted behind, carrying a load of happy caterflies on his fur. Poor Sassafras would be lonely without those caterfly cuddles!

"You dig up the dead plants and a good bit of the soil around them as well," Mom instructed. "All the thawing snow and rain we had a few weeks ago helped flush out most of the salt, but it's best to be safe. I'll add some fresh soil around each of the new catnip plants." Mom nodded her head toward the huge bag of potting soil we'd hauled in the wagon.

We worked and worked, and finally I patted the soil around the last baby catnip plant and sat down to admire our work.

"Don't you think Sassafras is doing a good job not drooling on the catnip?" I asked. I looked around for Sassafras. "Wait. Where is Sassafras?"

Mom and I scanned the area and found

Sassafras sitting completely still in front of a new plant.

"What is he doing?" I asked. As I got closer to investigate, I saw that he was cross-eyed. Staring at his nose.

I almost fell over laughing. Smack in the middle of Sassafras' nose was a tiny purring caterpillar. It was kneading his nose with its tiny caterpillar legs.

"They hatched!" I exclaimed to my mom. She rushed over and laughed when she saw poor Sassafras frozen in place.

"Wait!" I exclaimed, and Mom stopped in her tracks. I rummaged through my backpack. Ta-da! My camera. This would be the perfect photo! I had to hold my breath so the camera would stop shaking from my giggles. I took the photo and then coaxed the baby caterpillar onto my finger.

Sassafras let out a sigh of relief once his nose was caterpillar-free.

"He's so tiny!" I cooed. I rubbed his furry back and he purred. "Oh my gosh! He's soooo cute!"

I let Mom have a turn holding him, and after we set him on a catnip leaf, we watched in awe as he gobbled one leaf, then another, and another.

"Wow. They really eat a lot, don't they?" I asked Mom.

"Yep! It's a good thing we had the greenhouse to get the new catnip plants growing quickly."

"How can he fit so much food in that tiny little body?" I muttered as I squinted down at him.

"Ah, he can't. So he'll shed his skin several times, and each time, he'll get remarkably bigger. Just like a regular caterpillar."

"And like mayfly nymphs?" I asked. My mind wandered back to the merhorses we helped last summer. We needed to visit them now that the weather was warming up!

"Yes, just like the mayfly nymphs."

I shivered. "I'm glad I just grow. Shedding my skin to get bigger would be super gross."

Mom laughed. "Well, then it's a good thing you aren't an insect! Once they're big enough, the caterpillars will form chrysalises and their body parts will reorganize inside to form caterflies."

I made a face. Reorganizing body parts? Ew.

"All that talk about shedding skin and whatnot has probably made you hungry." Mom winked at me mischievously. "Let's get cleaned up for dinner."

We said a quick good-bye to the caterflies, who fluttered around the baby caterpillars to make sure they were safe and well-fed. Sassafras looked longingly back at the caterflies, and the catnip, and then joined us on the path toward home.

A KNOCK?
CHAPTER 14

Sassafras watched me check on my African violet babies at the dining room table from the safety of my lap. I carefully brushed the soil away from the leaf stem I'd planted in the dirt and lifted the leaf out. Yes! I could see tiny little nubs starting to grow at the bottom of the stems.

I dangled the leaf in front of Sassafras' face. "Look! Baby roots! My friends are going to freak out when I show them that I made a leaf grow into a new plant."

Sassafras blinked in agreement, then whipped his head to the side, and pointed his ears toward the kitchen.

"Meow?"

"Do you hear something, Sass?" I strained my ears. I didn't hear anything.

Sassafras leaped out of my lap and ran for the back door.

I followed, still straining to hear any noise.

Sassafras meowed impatiently and stretched his front legs up to the doorknob.

"Maybe someday you'll be able to open doors. But for now, how about I help you?" I grinned at him and twisted the doorknob.

There on the doorstep was a bundle of catnip. With a teeny tiny note attached. I picked it up and took a look:

A big smile spread across my face. "I believe these are for you, Sassafras," I said, bending down.

Sassafras took a step toward the catnip. "Meow?" He looked up at me.

"Yes, go ahead! It's yours!" I waved him on.

He dissolved into a writhing, purring, drooling mess of happiness.

I looked again at the miniature note and saw a tiny paw print. That was sweet of the caterflies—I couldn't believe they had so much catnip to spare. Unless . . . unless . . .

"Sassafras!" I shouted.

He looked up at me. Some drool and crumpled catnip leaves were smeared down one side of his face.

"The caterpillars! They must have made their chrysalises! That's why they don't need the catnip anymore. We've got to see them!"

"Meooow!" Sassafras cried and pawed at the pile of wet catnip.

"OK, two more minutes. Then I really want to go see." I looked at the note one more time and realized I should add it to my science journal before it got lost. It was just too cute.

I went to my room and glued it next to my entry on caterflies, across from that silly photo of Sassafras with the tiny caterpillar on his nose. I leaned in close to the photo and could barely make out the faint purrs of the caterpillar. I couldn't wait to see the chrysalises they'd made! I leaped up and rushed past my desk. The whoosh of air flipped my journal open to a new page.

A blank page, just waiting for whatever creature we'd help next . . .

GLOSSARY

Camouflage: When the natural coloring of an animal blends into its surroundings, which makes it harder for predators to find them.

Chrysalis: A life stage that comes after a caterpillar but before a butterfly or moth.

Freezing point: When a liquid turns to a solid. The freezing point for water is 32 degrees Fahrenheit (0 degrees Celsius): that's when water turns to ice.

Host plant: Where a mother butterfly lays her eggs, and where the baby caterpillars eat. Different butterflies and moths have different host plants.

Nymph: A kind of baby insect.

Predator: A living thing that eats other living things for food.

ABOUT THE AUTHOR AND ILLUSTRATOR

ASIA CITRO used to be a science teacher, but now she plays at home with her two kids and writes books. When she was little, she had a cat just like Sassafras. He loved to eat bugs and always made her laugh (his favorite toy was a plastic human nose that he carried everywhere). Asia has also written three activity books: *150+ Screen-Free Activities for Kids, The Curious Kid's Science Book,* and *A Little Bit of Dirt*. She has yet to find a baby dragon in her backyard, but she always keeps an eye out, just in case.

MARION LINDSAY is a children's book illustrator who loves stories and knows a good one when she reads it. She likes to draw anything and everything but does spend a completely unfair amount of time drawing cats. Sometimes she has to draw dogs just to make up for it. She illustrates picture books and chapter books as well as painting paintings and designing patterns. Like Asia, Marion is always on the lookout for dragons and sometimes thinks there might be a small one living in the airing cupboard.

for activities and more visit
ZOEYANDSASSAFRAS.COM